The Day the Sky Fell Down

Written by Michaela Morgan

Illustrated by Jane Cope

A chick went walking
    one fine day.
When a nut fell down
    and the chick said, "HEY!"

"The sky is falling.
  What bad luck!"
He told the hen
  and she said, "Cluck!"

"The sky is falling!
   Oh no! Oh no!
We've got to run!
   We've got to go!"

They met a turkey.
   They told him too.
He started to cry,
   "Boo hoo! Boo hoo!"

They all went on,
    clucking and calling.
Then they told a goose.
    She started bawling.

"The sky is falling!
   What can we do?"
A fox came along
   and said, "Yoo-hoo!"

"The sky is falling!
  You must hide.
Here's my den.
  You can hide inside."

The chick hopped in.
The den was hot.
He saw a big, big fire
and a cooking pot.

"Ha ha!" said the fox.
"You've come to lunch!
Now I'll have
a chick to munch!

"Chicks are silly.
They know nothing at all.
The sky stays up.
It cannot fall!"

Then the hen stamped her foot.
The turkey joined in.
The goose stamped too. What a din!

They stamped and they stamped
   and they made such a din.
That bit by bit... the roof fell in.

The fox fell down.
The chick was free!
He was as happy
as a chick can be.